PEARL'S MAGICAL ADVENTURE

Written by Nicole Navarrete

Illustrated by Brooke Navarrete

ThePublishingRoom.com

D1366885

ABOUT THE AUTHOR

Nicole Navarrete is an elementary school teacher who has always had a love for writing and reading. She lives in New Jersey with her husband, Sergio and her children Haleye, Ethan and Brooke. Nicole has a bachelor's degree in English and a master's degree in Education.

ABOUT THE ILLUSTRATOR

Brooke Navarrete is a 5th grade middle school student. She loves to paint, draw, dance and spend time with her family and friends. She lives in New Jersey with her mom, dad, sister, and brother.

To my mom and dad, thank you for always fostering my love for books and writing.

To my husband, thank you for always being there to help me pursue my dream.

To Haleye, Ethan and Brooke, thank you for the inspiration to finally write this book.

Copyright © 2020 by Nicole Navarrete

All rights reserved.

No part of this book may be reproduced or used in any manner without written permission of the copyright owner except for the use of quotations in a book review. For more information, address:

nicolenavarretebooks@gmail.com

FIRST EDITION

ThePublishingRoom.com

On a very cold winter day, Pearl the Penguin was waddling around the North Pole. Christmas was in two weeks and everyone was busy.

Pearl went to Santa's workshop to try to find her friend, Earl the Elf. She ran right into Santa. "Whoa, where are you going so fast," exclaimed Santa.

"Sorry Santa, It's so cold outside. I'm looking for Earl so we can warm up with some hot chocolate," Pearl replied.

"Ho, Ho, Ho, hot chocolate sounds so good right now. I need a break, I'm going to join you," Santa said.

They found Earl in the break room with a few of the other elves.

"Earl, we have been looking for you. Would you like to join me and Santa for a cup of hot chocolate?" asked Pearl.

Earl said, "Sure, that sounds delicious."

"I have the best hot chocolate in my office, let's go," said Santa.

"This hot chocolate is really warming me up. It is so cold out there," Pearl exclaimed.

"Last year, Mrs. Claus and I went on vacation to the beach. The weather was so warm," Santa told Pearl and Earl.

"Tell me more!" said Pearl.

Santa told Pearl all about his fantastic time at the beach, swimming in the ocean, building sandcastles and walking the boardwalk.

9

Then Pearl had the perfect idea. She wanted to know what it was like living on the beach, she was so tired of being cold.

She asked Santa, "Please let me go to the beach. I want to go live where it is warm"

11

Santa told Pearl, "If you go to the beach, you will have no friends there."

Pearl answered, "I will make new friends, I want to go."

"But your kind of penguin lives in the cold," Earl said.

Pearl was getting mad, she said, "I will be fine."

Then the head elf rushed in and yelled, "Santa, there's an emergency with the doll machine. Hurry, we need your help"

Earl and Pearl were left alone in Santa's office. Pearl reached for Santa's magic dust.

Earl said, "Pearl, what are you doing? You can't touch Santa's things."

Pearl replied, "I am going to the beach," as she sprinkled the magic dust on herself.

She exclaimed, "I wish to go to the beach where it's warm."

Next thing she knew, Pearl was on the beach. The water was in front of her and sand all around.

She said to herself, "What should I do first?"

She decided to build a sandcastle. She got all her tools together and got right to work. Every time she tried to build a part of the castle, it collapsed.

"What am I doing wrong," she thought.

She got really frustrated with the castle and turned to ask one of her friends for help. She then realized that none of her friends were there to help her. She started to cry, but then she thought, "I'll walk the boardwalk and go on some rides."

She couldn't wait to go on the ferris wheel, so she waited in line. She started to climb onto the ride and noticed how high the ferris wheel was. She thought, "I am afraid of heights, I can't do this alone. I wish Earl were here, he always gave me confidence."

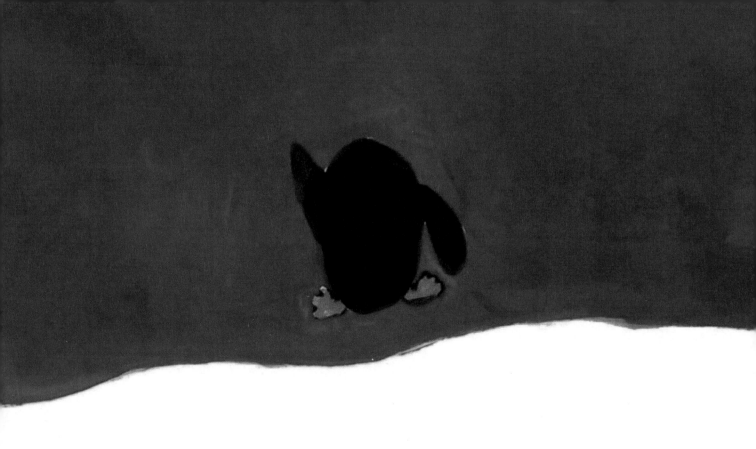

Pearl got off the ride and went back to the beach.

She said, "I know what I can do, I can go swimming."

She jumped right into the ocean and started swimming. As she was swimming, she remembered last time her and Earl went swimming and she missed him so much.

She thought, "What am I doing here? I need my friends."

She plopped on the sand and cried in frustration. She screamed loud for everyone to hear, "I want to go home to the North Pole."

Pearl ended up back in Santa's office. She saw Santa and Earl right away and ran up to them with a big hug. "I missed you so much, I never want to leave again, " Pearl exclaimed.

From then on, Pearl and Earl were happy doing everything at the North Pole together. Pearl never wanted to go on an adventure again without her friends.

Made in the USA
Middletown, DE
26 September 2020

20553840R00020